This book belongs to:

Dear readers,

In 1931, Tom Faber, who was not yet four, received a letter from his godfather, T. S. Eliot, telling of his 'Lilliecat' Jellylorum, whose one idea was to be USEFUL!! Enchanted, the young boy told his parents 'I think Uncle Tom's a very good writer'.

That little boy Tom Faber was my father. I like to think it was his godson's encouragement that encouraged T. S. Eliot to think he could write poems for children. So it was that various cat poems appeared in letters over the years, but it was not until 1939 that they were collected in the now world-famous Old Possum's Book of Practical Cats.

That might have been the end of the cat poems were it not for the arrival of Morgan, a very large, black cat who fastened himself on Faber's offices in Russell Square soon after the outbreak of the Second World War. Apparently Morgan would keep Tom Faber, T. S. Eliot and their colleagues company during the long night hours, as they watched for bombs from the roof of the publishing house.

In 1951, another poem appeared in which Cat Morgan introduced himself. For obvious reasons, it's one of my favourites among all Old Possum's poems. I hope you will like it as much as I do.

Toby Faber,
grandson of Geoffrey Faber (founder of Faber & Faber)

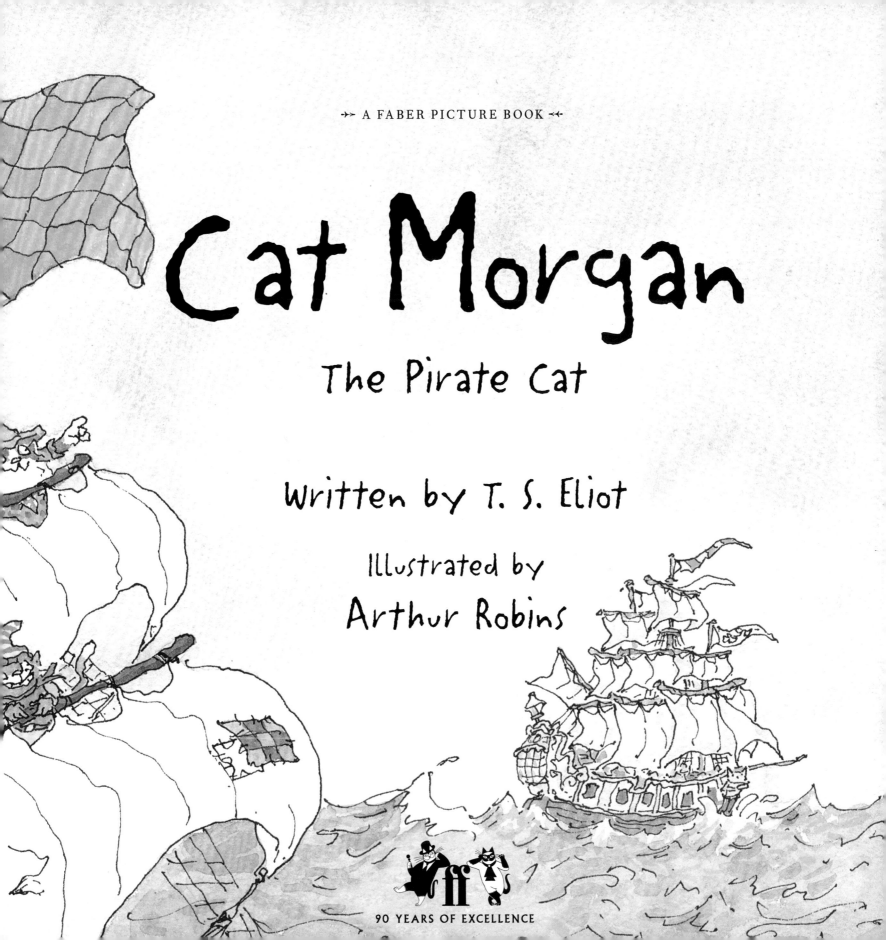

⇥ A FABER PICTURE BOOK ⇤

Cat Morgan

The Pirate Cat

Written by T. S. Eliot

Illustrated by

Arthur Robins

90 YEARS OF EXCELLENCE

I once was a Pirate
what sailed the 'igh seas—

But now I've retired
as a com-mission-aire:

And that's how you find me a-takin' my ease

And keepin' the door in a Bloomsbury Square.

I'm partial to partridges, likewise to grouse,

And I favour that Devonshire cream in a bowl;

But I'm allus content with a drink on the 'ouse

And a bit o' cold fish when I done me patrol.

I ain't got much polish, me manners is gruff,

But I've got a good coat, and I keep meself smart;

And everyone says, and I guess that's enough;

I got knocked about on the Barbary Coast,

And me voice it ain't no sich melliferous horgan;

But yet I can state, and I'm not one to boast,

That some of the gals is dead keen on old Morgan.

So if you 'ave business with Faber—or Faber—

I'll give you this tip, and it's worth a lot more:

You'll save yourself time,
and you'll spare yourself labour

If jist you make friends
with the Cat at the door.

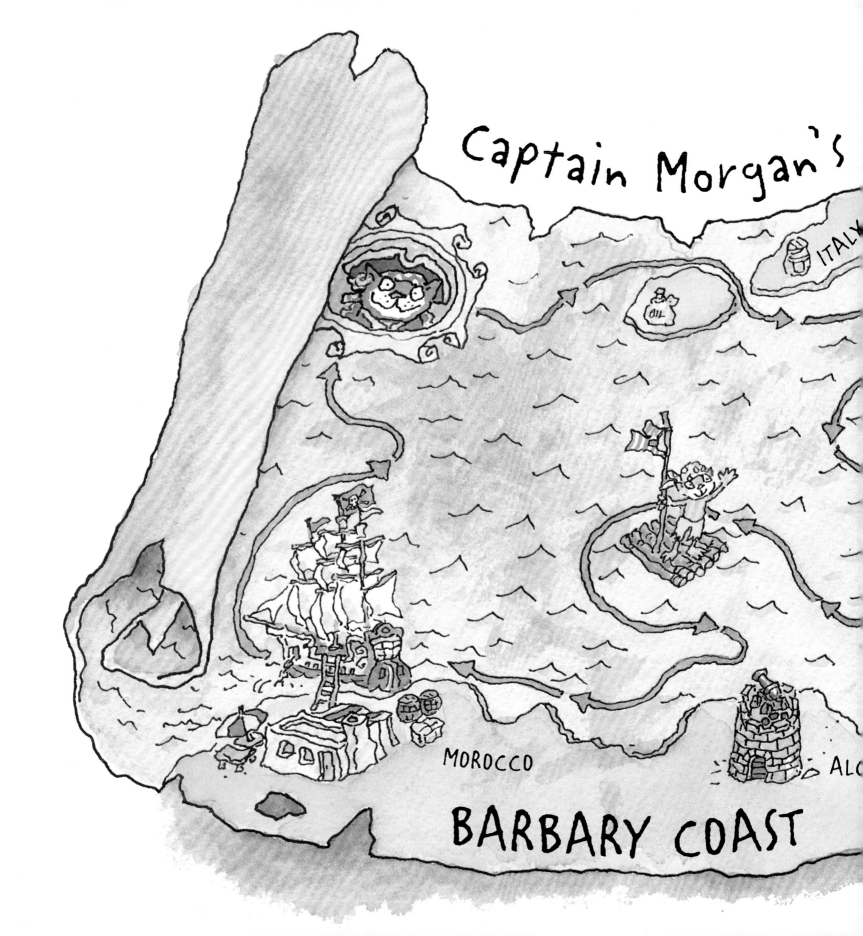

Captain Morgan's

ITALY

OIL

MOROCCO

ALG

BARBARY COAST

Expeditions

TRIPOLI

With thanks to Leah. A. R.

From the original collection,
'respectfully dedicated to those friends who have assisted its
composition by their encouragement, criticism and suggestions:
and in particular to Mr T. E. Faber, Miss Alison Tandy,
Miss Susan Wolcott, Miss Susanna Morley, and the Man in White Spats. O.P.'

First published in 1953 in the revised edition of Old Possum's Book of Practical Cats by Faber and Faber Ltd, Bloomsbury House, 74—77 Great Russell Street, London WC1b 3DA
This edition first published in 2019

Printed in china

A CIP record for this book is available from the British Library
ISBN 978-0-571-34582-3

2 4 6 8 10 9 7 5 3 1